Playtime at Grandma's House

To The Best
Orthodontist EVRR
Love A.L.Green-Williams
"Princess"
10/24/2019

A. L. Green-Williams

Ordering Information:

For orders and inquiries, please contact:
1-888-375-9818
www.toplinkpublishing.com
bookorder@toplinkpublishing.com

Printed in the United States of America

Dedication

Playtime at Grandma's House is dedicated to all of the grandparents who have been instrumental in their grand children's lives, and to the grand children who are blessed to share precious moments with their grand parents. To those children who have not experienced the extraordinary love from a grandparent, this book is dedicated to.Also to my granddaughter Whitlee, who is blessed to have many grandparents, I pray that you delight in our love, embrace our wisdom, and cherish every treasured moment you have with us.

To my husband, parents and family, this book is dedicated to you and all of the sacred moments you have shared with your grandparent, and with each other.

To an astounding writer who has inspired me for many years, Dr. Maya Angelou. I will never forget standing in line for two hours in Los Angeles at one of her book signings, and was gracefully greeted by her. Dr Maya Angelou's spirit lives on. Thank you for setting the stage for my writings.

I would like to thank Carol Bianchi for allowing me to take a photo of her mother's shed. Carol's mom, Edna (Eddie) Johnstone, passed away before she had the opportunity to 'play' in it, and I believe that she would have been very happy knowing that many others will as they read this book.

Lastly, but definitely not least. This book and all others yet to come is dedicated to my Lord, Jesus Christ, who is the author and finisher of my faith.

Hello my name is Whitlee. I love playtime at Grandma's house. I play with my dolls in the shed underneath the big avocado tree in Grandma's backyard.

The shed is my playhouse.

My dolls, Walking Wendy and Cathy Quick Curl, will play with Grandma and me today. Walking Wendy is tall with long brown hair, and when I hold Wendy's hand her legs move. Cathy Quick Curl is smaller with yellow wired hair, which makes it easier for me to comb in all sorts of curls

"Grandma, can we have a tea party today inside my playhouse?"

"Sure, we can, Whitlee."

Inside my playhouse is a white round table, four white chairs, and a red Easy Bake Oven.

I sit Wendy and Cathy on their very own chairs at the table.

"Wendy and Cathy, our playhouse needs some cleaning." As I'm sweeping the floor, Wendy and Cathy just watch me the entire time. Grandma comes in just as I finish.

"Whitlee, it looks really nice in here."

"Thank you, Grandma."

"I have tea for all of us. Girls, should we have cake to go with our tea?"

"Oh, yes, Grandma. We all want cake." It looks as though Wendy and Cathy are both happy with my decision

Grandma says, "Okay, Whitlee, let us get these hands washed,"

I also take Wendy and Cathy to get their hands washed.

Grandma says, "Is everyone washed up and ready for tea and cake?"

"Yes, we are Grandma." I show Grandma both sides of my hands, and the girls' hands, too."

"Whitlee, I'm going to sit down right here at the table with Wendy and Cathy, and watch you bake us a cake."

"Okay, Grandma." Grandma, Wendy, and Cathy are waiting anxiously for me to start baking.

I open the small cake box and empty it into a small bowl. Then I pour in the water, mix the ingredients together, and pour the mixture into a small baking pan. I place the pan inside my red Easy Bake Oven. The smell of cake fills my play house.

Grandma says, "Mmmmm Mmmmmm.
Girls, doesn't that cake smell good?"

Wendy smiles, and so does Kathy.

"Yes, Grandma. I want to eat it now."

When the cake is ready, Grandma pours the tea into four tiny tea cups. My tea set is trimmed in gold and is covered with pictures of butterflies, lady bugs, dragonflies, bees, and flowers.

Grandma cuts four small pieces of cake and places them on four small plates.

Grandma asks, "Whose turn is it to say grace? Is it yours, Wendy? Is it your turn, Cathy?"

"It's my turn, Grandma."

"I believe it is your turn, Whitlee."

"God is great, God is good,
thank you God for our food, Amen."

"Amen. Girls, let's dig in," says Grandma.

I eat my piece of cake, and Grandma eats hers, but I want more.

"Wendy, may I have your piece of cake, please?" Wendy smiles, and I eat Wendy's piece of cake.

"Cathy, may I have your piece of cake, please, please?" Cathy is so nice that she gives me her piece of cake.

"Thank you both for sharing your cake with me." "It's so good."

"Grandma, this is the best tea party ever, and you're the best Grandma in the whole wide world. Can we play jump rope?"

Grandma's Words of Wisdom

"I would like to have flowers while I can still smell them"

"Say what you need, and have faith that God will get it for you"

"Do unto others, as you would have them do unto you"

"Don't forget to come in when the street lights come on"

"Treat others the way you would like to be treated"

'If you don't have anything good to say about someone, then don't

say anything at all"

"Be polite, and always respect your elders"

"Always act like a lady and cross your legs"

"Think before you speak"

CPSIA information can be obtained
at www.ICGtesting.com
Printed in the USA
BVHW021630070419
544795BV00002B/12/P